THE
WIDOW'S
BROOM

CHRIS VAN ALLSBURG

A SCHOLASTIC EDITION

To My Friend Maurice

ISBN 0-590-47543-6

12 11 10 9 8 7 6 5 4 3 2 1   3 4 5 6 7 8/9

Printed in the U.S.A.   37

First Scholastic printing, October 1993

THE
WIDOW'S
BROOM

Witches' brooms don't last forever. They grow old, and even the best of them, one day, lose the power of flight.

Fortunately, this does not happen in an instant. A witch can feel the strength slowly leaving her broom. The sudden bursts of energy that once carried her quickly into the sky become weak. Longer and longer running starts are needed for takeoff. Speedy brooms that, in their youth, outraced hawks are passed by slow flying geese. When these things happen, a witch knows it's time to put her old broom aside and have a new one made.

On very rare occasions, however, a broom can lose its power without warning, and fall, with its passenger, to the earth below . . . which is just what happened one cold autumn night many years ago.

Out of a moonlit sky a dark cloaked figure came spinning to the ground. The witch, along with her tired broom, landed beside a small white farmhouse, the home of a lonely widow named Minna Shaw.

At daybreak, Widow Shaw discovered the witch lying in her vegetable garden. She was bruised and bloody and couldn't stand up on her own. In spite of her fear, and because she was a kind woman, Minna Shaw helped the witch inside and put her to bed.

The witch asked Minna Shaw to draw the curtains, then wrapped herself tightly in her black cape and fell soundly asleep. She lay there, perfectly still, all day and all evening. When she finally awoke at midnight, her wounds had completely healed.

She rose from the bed and moved silently through the widow's house. Minna Shaw was asleep in a chair by the fireplace, where embers of a dying fire glowed on the hearth. The witch knelt and took one of the red hot coals in her hand.

Outside she made a fire of leaves and twigs, then dropped a strand of her hair into the flame. The fire hissed and crackled, burning with a brilliant blue light.

Before long the witch could see a dark form flying overhead. It was another witch, who circled slowly and landed beside the fire. The two women spoke briefly, the first witch gesturing toward the garden where her old broom rested. Then they sat side by side on the second witch's broom and flew off, over the treetops.

When Minna Shaw woke up she wasn't surprised to find that her guest had gone. Witches, she knew, had unusual powers.

It didn't surprise her either when she saw that the old broom had been left behind. The widow guessed it had lost its magic. It was an ordinary broom now, just like the one she kept in her kitchen. She began using it around the house and found that it was no better or worse than brooms she'd used before.

One morning Minna Shaw was still in bed when she heard a noise coming from the kitchen. She peeked in and saw something that made her heart jump. There was the broom, sweeping the floor all by itself. It stopped for a moment and turned to the widow, then went back to work.

At first Minna was frightened, but the broom seemed harmless, and, what's more, it was doing a very good job. Unfortunately, it swept all day long.

In the evening, to get some peace, she locked the broom in a closet, but when it tapped on the door for more than an hour Minna felt guilty and let it out. As she lay in bed listening to the broom sweeping each room over and over, she wondered if it could learn to do other things.

In the morning she led the broom outside and found out that it was a very good student. She needed to show it how to do something only once. Soon the broom could chop wood and fetch water, feed the chickens and bring the cow in from the pasture. It could even pick out simple tunes on the piano.

Soon, more distant neighbors heard about the broom and visited the widow's farm. The men who saw it seemed to agree, it probably was a wicked thing. But their wives pointed out that it was a great help to the widow and could play the piano well, considering that it struck just one note at a time. No one's feelings were as strong as Mr. Spivey's. "It's evil and it's dangerous," he told everyone who would listen. "We'll all be sorry if this thing stays among us."

As days went by, the broom seemed as innocent and hardworking as ever. Though it had learned how to do many things, sweeping brought it special pleasure. It was, after all, a broom. Occasionally, when there was nothing left to do around the widow's house, it would hop down to the road that separated Minna Shaw's and the Spiveys' farms. The road was dirt, of course, and the broom could amuse itself there for hours.

One afternoon two of the Spivey boys and their dog walked along the road where the broom was happily at work. When they saw what it was doing, they kicked the small stones the broom had swept aside back into its path. The broom ignored them and shuffled off to sweep another part of the road.

But the Spivey boys would not leave it alone. They called the broom names. When it continued to ignore them, they picked up a couple of sticks and started tapping the broom's handle.

Finally, it stopped sweeping. The broom turned to the two boys and knocked them both on the head so hard they fell to the ground in tears. The broom hopped off, but the Spivey dog ran after it, yapping and biting at its bristles. "Get him!" the boys yelled. The little dog leaped into the air and caught the broom by the handle. But he was not there for long.

That evening Mr. Spivey drove his wagon up to the widow's house. He was not alone. Three men from neighboring farms were in the wagon, along with a long wooden stake and coils of rope.

Mr. Spivey knocked loudly. When she opened her door, Minna was frightened by what she saw. "We've come for the broom," her neighbor told her. "It's beaten my sons and likely done worse to my dog." The poor animal was nowhere to be found.

The widow could tell by their faces that the men would not be leaving without her broom. There was nothing she could do to stop them. For a moment she stood silently, then answered. "Of course you are right. If it could do such a thing, we must get rid of it."

She led the men into her kitchen. "It sleeps in here," she whispered, pointing to a closet. "If you move it carefully, it will not wake up." The men knew how strong the broom was and hoped the widow was right.

They opened the closet door, revealing the slumbering broom. One of the farmers took it out and gently held it against the stake while the others wrapped it in yards of rope.

They carried the broom outside, drove the stake into the ground, and gathered straw around it. Mr. Spivey lit the fire. In no time, flames turned the broom to ashes.

Life soon returned to normal around the widow's farm. The Spiveys even found their dog, healthy but hungry, caught in the branches of a tall spruce tree.

Then one morning Minna Shaw called on her neighbors with frightening news. She had seen the ghost of the broom. It was as white as snow and moved through the woods at night carrying an axe. Mr. Spivey did not believe her. But that night, under a full moon, he watched from a window as the broom's white ghost came out of the woods and slowly circled his house. The next night it returned, circling even closer, and the night after it came again, tapping the axe lightly on the Spiveys' door.

The next morning Mr. and Mrs. Spivey packed their dearest possessions and eight children into their wagon. Mr. Spivey tried to convince the widow to leave with them, but she chose to stay behind in her little farmhouse. She went down to the road as the wagon pulled away and waved good-bye to her neighbors. "You're a brave woman!" Mr. Spivey called out.

That evening the widow fell asleep in her chair by the fire. She'd been listening to music, simple tunes played one note at a time on the piano. A gentle tap on the shoulder woke her. She looked up and smiled at the broom, not a ghost at all, but still covered with the coat of white paint she'd given it.

"You play so nicely," Minna Shaw said. The broom bowed, put a log on the fire, and played another tune.

The type is set in Simoncini Garamond by Monotype Composition.
Camera work by CAIRAgraphics Company, Inc.
The paper is Monadnock Text supplied by Monadnock Paper Mills, Inc.
Both text and jacket are printed by Mercantile Printing Company, Inc.
The books are bound by Horowitz/Rae.